The

Little

Boy

By Rohan Hall

For information, contact:
Eye Contact Media, Inc.
www.eyecontactmedia.com
info@eyecontactmedia.com

ISBN 10: 0-9729187-5-2
ISBN 13: 978-0-9729187-5-6
Printed in Hong Kong

Dedicated

To the perfect child in all of us

I woke up feeling a bit sad this morning. The sun was shining, but the world seemed dark. I knew I had many good things in my life, yet for some reason I still felt blue. I had a good job to go to, but yet I just didn't feel like getting up.

My wonderful wife lay next to me, but I just wasn't feeling love. I asked myself: *How can I be so sad when I have so much?*

That's when I remembered the story of the little boy.

This is a story I first heard when I was young. It has helped me on many occasions through the years when I felt lost and distant from the world.

No one knows how the story started or who told it first.

I'm only telling it now under one condition: If
you find faith and happiness from the story,
you must share it with others.

I love telling the story, because it always helps
me remember why I should be happy.

The story of the little boy

The little boy woke up in a strange mood one morning. He didn't know what was wrong with him, but he felt sad and the sadness wouldn't go away. He walked around for a long time with his face in a frown.

He went to school and worked hard, but most of the other kids seemed to have better grades, no matter how hard he tried. He felt average. He wanted to be gifted like some of the other children. He wanted to win prizes and have his papers hang on the wall for everyone to admire.

At home, he tried to play with his toys, but they didn't interest him. He felt too sad for play.

"What's wrong?" his mother asked.
"You seem sad lately."

"I am sad," the little boy answered. "But I don't know why. I just feel sad."

She smiled at him. "But you have so much to be happy about! Don't you know you're a perfect child of God?"

"The teacher at school says we're not perfect," he responded.

His mother shook her head. "Your teacher's wrong about that.
You're my son, so I know. You're a child of God—and God never makes mistakes."

The boy frowned, thinking about her words. "Well, if I'm perfect, then why am I so sad?"

"You're simply lost," said his mother. "You've lost your vision of all the things you've been given by your father"

"What do you mean?" he replied.

She sat beside him and pulled him close "I'll tell you a story—the first story ever made. It's about the first children and how they got lost."

The little boy snuggled against her, already

feeling better.

"Okay," he said with a smile. "I love

stories." And so he heard the tale of the

first lost children.

The Story of Adam and Eve

In the beginning there were no people living on Earth, so God created two children and named them Adam and Eve.

Adam and Eve were the light of the world. God was proud of them and knew that through them he had extended his perfection.

He also knew that each time he looked at them he would see a vision of himself. So into them he poured all his love and passion and dreams and hopes.

The children were happy and enjoyed all the gifts of the world.

They had a beautiful silver moon to light the sky at night.

They were given a warm sun, which reminded them that they are the light of the world, and they had rich, beautiful earth in which to plant the seeds of life.

The blue-green ocean was also theirs—

a reminder of the womb from which

they were born, the sacred giver of life.

The wind filled their lungs with clean, sweet air, and the birds sang beautiful songs.

The world was filled with plenty and it was good.

In return, God asked for nothing. But he

wanted them to remember two things:

- Appreciate all the gifts of the world

  or it shall be taken from you.

- Happiness is Godliness.

Appreciate the gifts of God

After awhile, the children became bored and forgot the lessons taught to them by God.

Adam and Eve played by the river with stones, but they wanted other things to do.

They climbed the trees, and when the trees weren't high enough, they climbed the tallest mountains.

They swam in the deep ocean and played with the fishes, but they didn't appreciate these gifts.

One day they felt a great sadness come over them, so they spoke to God.

God told them, "Appreciate the gifts of the world or they shall be taken away from you."

"Show me how!" Adam responded.
So God held Adam's hand and walked
through the dirt with Adam and Eve.

"Do you feel the dirt under your bare toes?
This dirt is the foundation of all life. Touch
it, feel it, and use it to grow things so your
children may live forever."

God took a deep breath and continued.
"Breathe the air deep into your lungs. This
air is my essence and it always surrounds
you, as I do."

He touched a tree. "Eat from the fruits of
my trees. They provide the fuel needed for
life.

This and so much more I've provided

for you. Open your eyes and enjoy all

that's here for you, today and every

day. It's all yours. Only when you

don't see these things will you feel as if

you have nothing. Remember this."

He continued. "Every day you should acknowledge and appreciate the things that are important to your life. Through this appreciation of the world around you, you'll find happiness and be closer to me. Remember, your happiness is a reflection of my love for you."

Holding the little boy in her arms, his mother finished the story.

"So God taught Adam and Eve that it isn't what you have that makes you happy—it's the appreciation of what you have. Your happiness makes God happy and shines God's love unto the world."

The boy asked, "So I need to appreciate everything I have?"

His mother nodded. "Yes, son. Let's make a list of the wonderful things in your life."

The boy thought for a few minutes as he

pictured his life. Here's the list he made:

My Happy List

- My mommy and daddy love me.

- I'm healthy and not sick.

- I have nice friends to play with.

- I have a new game that's fun.

- I get to play in the park later.

Before long they'd listed a page full of things the little boy was grateful for. He then promised to add more to the list every day.

He put the paper beside his bed where he could see it each morning.

Every day he added new things to the list,

and whenever he felt sad he read it again.

He learned how lucky he was. He also

learned how fortunate he was to be such a

perfect little boy.

After I remembered this story, I looked
around the room. When had I forgotten
it? How had I lost my way? This wasn't
the first time I'd forgotten God's love,
and each time, thinking of the story
helped me find my way.

I asked God to help me find happiness and to see the beauty of the world. This was the lesson I'd learned from that little boy.

Sometimes we see only what's wrong with our lives and with the world and that is the only thing we can focus on.

We forget to be happy about the many wonderful things that we have in our lives. We forget to appreciate life itself.

I took a paper and started writing a list of the wonderful things in my life. Writing gives life to what we feel.

Where I thought I had nothing to be happy about, I now found I couldn't stop writing.

Now, sunlight seemed to cover the walls in the room. The plant itself felt alive. The burden I'd felt only moments ago seemed to drift away from my body.

Instead of seeing only what was wrong

with me, I could now see what was right.

I smiled as I read my list. I'd written

things I hadn't thought about in years—

little things I'd forgotten.